Foreword

This is a book of two sections.

The first section is "Ellie's Magical Cat". A story to stir the imagination and emotions of young readers and young-at-heart adults.

If this inspires you to try dancing, or build on what you know, you may care to read the "Goddard Method of Latin Dancing" in the second section of the book. (Possibly of more interest to older children and adults, but suitable for any age.)

Happy reading 😊

Copyright James Goddard 2022

Ellie's Magical Cat – Adventures Through the Cat's Shadow

After her beloved husband passed away, Ellie was lonely, so she got a cat as company.

Ellie called the cat 'Hugo' after her late husband as she thought the cat and Hugo looked a bit alike because they both had grey hair.

Hugo used to call Ellie 'Coco' as a nickname when she was younger before her hair turned grey.

Hugo and Ellie had met through a shared love of dancing. They fell in love, got married and lived happily together for years. They didn't have any children.

Ellie felt very sad after her husband Hugo died. She had moved to a smaller house and no longer had room for all the items that she and Hugo had bought together.

Now all she had in the world to remember him by were some pictures. Plus Hugo the cat.

Ellie kept herself occupied with various hobbies and activities during the daytime, but in the evenings could find herself thinking about their life together.

One night when Ellie went to bed, she found herself thinking about her cat and her husband Hugo.

Hugo the cat lay on the bed next to Ellie, purring softly and trying to gently sooth her towards sleep.

However, Ellie didn't sleep. When she looked out of the window the moonlight seemed particularly bright and gave Ellie a funny feeling that made her tingle all over. She wasn't sure if she was dreaming or if there was magic in the air.

In the moonlight the cat's shadow crept along the bed up the wall until it touched a picture of Hugo that Ellie had hung on the wall. The cat's shadow turned into a man's silhouette – Hugo's!

It seemed that her husband had come back! He stood beside Ellie's bed and silently offered her his hand. He had an enormous grin on his face just like she remembered.

Hugo was wearing a tuxedo. Ellie was wearing a formal ball gown which she did not remember putting on. The clock on the bedside table said 10pm so no time appeared to have passed since she had last looked at the clock.

Strangely Hugo's face was no longer in the picture on the wall....

....stranger still, Hugo and Ellie seemed to be young again, somewhere in their twenties or thirties.

Ellie wasn't sure if she was dreaming. She took Hugo's hand and they started dancing around the floor.

Without any apparent effort they rose from the floor and circled around the room 'tripping the light fantastic' as Hugo used to say when they danced really well together. Two people moving as one, following one another's footsteps with ease. It was graceful and beautiful to watch.

Hugo and Ellie danced out of the window into the night sky.

Hugo and Ellie flew from building to building dancing in the moon lit sky. It seemed to last for hours.

Lost in the moment there seemed no need to speak. Hugo and Ellie danced smoothly together seeming to travel across the sky gliding from roof top to roof top. It reminded Ellie of the feeling when she was floating in water at the swimming pool. Every part of her felt calm and supported.

They slipped from one dance style to another. Their mood seemed to set the dance they chose. A casual walk became a waltz in the air between buildings. A game of hide and seek amongst the roof tops became a jive. Another walk in the sky between buildings turned into a relaxed social foxtrot. They carried on like this for some time.

Hugo brought Ellie back to her room after their adventure dancing across the night sky.

"Hugo, there's something I want to ask you" said Ellie as they hovered outside her house near her bedroom window. "Why have you come back? I have really missed you, but I don't understand how, or where you came from?"

Hugo looked puzzled then thoughtful. "Who knows, but let's enjoy the moment." Hugo's rueful mood became more upbeat as his positive nature re-established itself. Perhaps because he hoped he would come back another evening.

A cloud passed over the moon and created a shadow. Everything went black, then Ellie woke up in bed. Had she just seen Hugo or was it all just a hopeful dream???

Several nights after Ellie had first danced in the sky with Hugo, she wondered if she had dreamt it all. As nothing had happened for several nights she thought of the event as a pleasant whimsy and put it to the back of her mind.

Ellie went for a late evening walk as usual. Night was falling so it was dark when she returned home. She met Hugo the cat who followed her back down the street to their house.

Under the light of a street lamp the cat's shadow appeared to turn from a cat into a man's silhouette – Hugo's! His shadow's hands appeared to be holding Ellie's.

Ellie was too surprised to say anything other than "Hugo, you've come back!" Instinctively she pulled Hugo towards her and hugged him fiercely, not wanting to lose him again. Their sense of joy made them want to dance.

Feeling young and full of energy Ellie wanted to do a quickstep, something she had always thought of as a happy dance, which somehow seemed appropriate.

Ellie realised not only did she feel young at heart, but she was young again, and so was Hugo.

Ellie felt as though she was dancing on air as Hugo took her in his arms and they danced the quickstep just as they used to.

At first they joyfully danced around the street, then Ellie suddenly realised they were dancing on air as they rose into the sky and glided elegantly through the air with a foxtrot. The initial excitement had naturally led to Ellie wondering how the situation occurred, so the speed of dancing slowed to reflect her thoughtful mood. Hugo and Ellie sailed from cloud to cloud and circled over the town.

As they danced around the sky, Hugo and Ellie travelled over places they had visited together, and happy memories came flooding back.

Ellie remembered the time she and Hugo had visited......

....the aquarium and seen the fishes....

.... the cinema to see a film....

....their favourite restaurant to enjoy a meal together.

Remembering their favourite restaurant Hugo and Ellie drifted lower, hand in hand to look more closely.

Ellie felt hungry after all their dancing together. She wondered if she and Hugo could get a meal together. She looked forward to spending time with him just like the old days, she missed him so much!

A cloud passed overhead, between the moon and Hugo and Ellie who were floating near the restaurant entrance.

Because the moon was hidden Hugo began to grow dim then transparent. He gently let go of Ellie and backed away smiling sadly. "It looks as though our time together is over for now" he said.

With Hugo gone, there seemed nothing to hold Ellie at the restaurant. Like a ship free of its anchor, or an aeroplane free of the ground, Ellie appeared to fly back to her room.

Ellie found herself wide awake in bed staring up at the ceiling. She asked herself if she had just dreamed her adventure with Hugo or if it somehow had happened? If so, how? Could there be such a thing as magic? That only happened in stories and this was real life....

Ellie was not sure if or when she would ever see Hugo again. She had a strong feeling that when the cat's shadow was created by a patch of light, and Ellie was thinking of her husband Hugo, then the magic could happen....

After all, love is a strong, powerful and magical force. If you wish hard enough, dreams sometimes come true....

The End....???

Ellie's dream…. she wonders if Hugo lives on through her cat???

Acknowledgements

Susanna West Yates and Tony Cronshaw

Thank you for all your help and support as editors.

Proof Readers

Thank you for all your proof reading: Amy, Sarah, Claire, James H., Eleanor and Leslie.

Illustrator

'ankaramedia' – Thank you so much for your hard work and drawing so many high-quality illustrations.

Cover Designer

'art_place' – Thank you so much for the design. I hope readers find it eye catching.

Book Promotion

'princessmarketr'– Thank you for technical advice on marketing.

About the Author

James Goddard

This book is James' first published fiction book. Please enjoy! ☺

James has written several non-fiction books to help children and adults how to learn how to dance and do martial arts. These are available on Amazon and Kindle under 'Goddard Method'.

James noticed there were patterns and crossovers in principles of movements in dancing and martial arts. This is what inspired him to write his books.

You can find out details about, and specials offers for, James' books on https://jamesgoddarddancing.wordpress.com

The Goddard Method of
LATIN DANCING
Lockdown Edition
by James Goddard
Quick wins to
make you look
and feel great.
For beginners
and experienced
dancers.

Foreword

Introducing the Goddard Method of Latin Dancing

Foreword on the Goddard Method of Latin Dancing

After Covid-19 Lockdown, now could be a good time to try new hobbies or practice an old one with your other half.

This is a series of guides that can be used (in lockdown or at other times) as quick introductions to dances for beginners or aide memoirs of key points for more experienced dancers.

It may be difficult to find space to do Ballroom dances. Latin dances can be done in a large room or conservatory [indoors]; or [outside] on a flat surface such as a patio.

Dancing is walking to music. A common mistake in dancing is that people try to move unnaturally (eg stiffly) looking at their feet and leaning on someone else. When dancing, move naturally as you would when walking with a friend:

- Fall into step and go to the same place at the same time.
- Move in the same general direction as other people.
- Don't barge into others.
- Don't expect other people to prop you up.

In order to dance you will need to dance the correct steps to the correct rhythm, whilst leading or following.

How do I know which way to go? As a rule of thumb for Latin dancing: Stay in one place, at least for moves in these guides. (Except for the Paso Doble. There can be some travel in dances like the Samba when using more advanced moves eg running promenades.)

All dances in the following guides start with the Leader's left foot and Follower's right foot, except for the Paso Doble and Samba, which start with Leader's right foot and Follower's left foot. The illustrations assume the man is the Leader.

All dance steps shown in these guides are performed in the standard 'teapot' hold (framework) unless indicated otherwise.

The framework is called 'teapot' as one arm is bent and the other more or less straight, but this can vary in position for Latin dances.

This is a typical Latin framework (gap between dancers' bodies).

Body contact is vital in leading and following:

- Form a framework of two points of contact (hand and arm).
- Maintain the framework (Leader and Follower hold on to each other) for the entire dance.

On the following pages are a series of guides to get you dancing Latin steps.

- Cha Cha Cha.
- Jive.
- Paso Doble.
- Rumba.
- Samba.

Cha Cha Cha Basic Steps

Basic Step (Rock Step and Chasse)
New York Step
Hand to Hand Step
Alemana (Underarm Turn)

Cha Cha Cha Basic Steps

Key principles for dancing the Cha Cha Cha:

1) The steps are:

- Step.
- Rock.
- Side.
- Close.
- Side.

2) The basic steps rhythm is always 2, 3, 4 and 1. This can vary in more advanced moves.

Suggested routine:

- *Basic Step.*
- *New York.*
- *Basic Step.*
- *Hand to Hand.*
- *Alemana* (underarm turn).

Basic Step (Rock Step and Chasse)

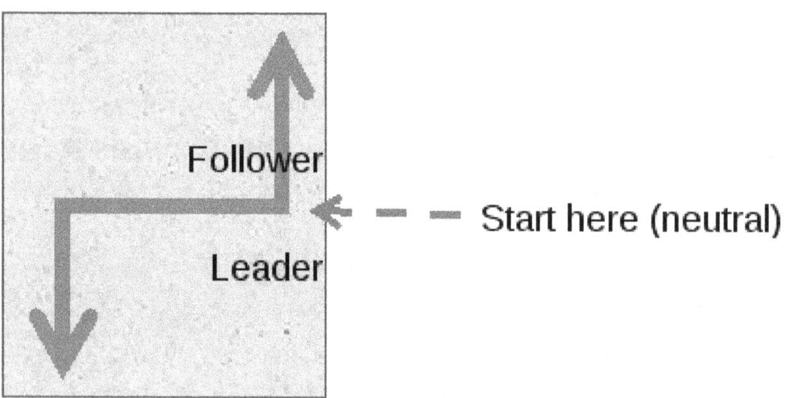

This is like going from third to second gear and back when driving a car.

Leader: Step forward towards "third gear" > Rock back > Side > Close > Side > Step backward towards "second gear" > Rock forward > Side > Close > Side.

Follower: Step backwards towards "third gear" > Rock forward > Side > Close > Side > Step forward towards "second gear" > Rock back > Side > Close > Side.

New York Step

This is performed from a two-handed grip, instead of the usual teapot framework, whilst going side to side.

Leader: Step forward towards right side > Rock back > (Face partner) side > Close > Side > Step forward left side > Rock backward > (Face partner) side > Close > Side.

Follower: Step forward left side > Rock backward > (Face partner) side > Close > Side > Step forward towards right side > Rock back > (Face partner) side > Close > Side.

Hand to Hand Step

This is performed from a two-handed grip, instead of the usual teapot framework, whilst going side to side.

It is the mirror image off an *New York* step, so step backwards instead of forwards.

Leader: Step backward towards right side > Rock forward > (Face partner) side > Close > Side > Step backward left side > Rock forward > (Face partner) side > Close > Side.

Follower: Step backward towards left side > Rock forward > (Face partner) side > Close > Side > Step backward right side > Rock back > (Face partner) side > Close > Side.

Alemana (Underarm Turn)

This is usually done after another step eg a basic (*Rock Step* and *Chasse*).
Stay in teapot framework except for the underarm turn.

The Leader raises his/her left hand (holding Follower's right), above the Leader's left shoulder (equi-distant between Leader and Follower); and uses the Leader's right hand on Follower's left hip to help the Follower turn under the Leader's hand.

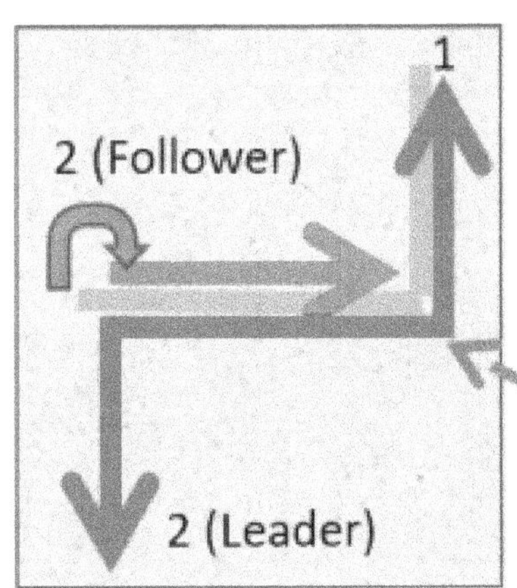

Leader: *(Basic Step (1))* step forward > Rock backward > Side > Close > Side > *(Alemana (2))* step backward, lift arm for Follower to turn under > Rock forward > Side > Close > Side.

Follower: Step backward > Rock forward > Side > Close > Side > Cross left foot over right > 360 degree clockwise turn under Leader's raised arm to face partner again > Side > Close > Side.

To improve your spins, think: Turn (beat 2) > Turn (beat 3) > Rebalance then step, step, step (beats 4 and 1).

Fan and Hockey Stick

Fan - Direction of Travel

Imagine a clock dial.

We will travel: Centre > 12 > Centre > 9 > Centre > 12.

Key

Red Follower's steps

Grey Leader's steps

Blue Both dancers change the

direction you are facing

during the *Fan* move

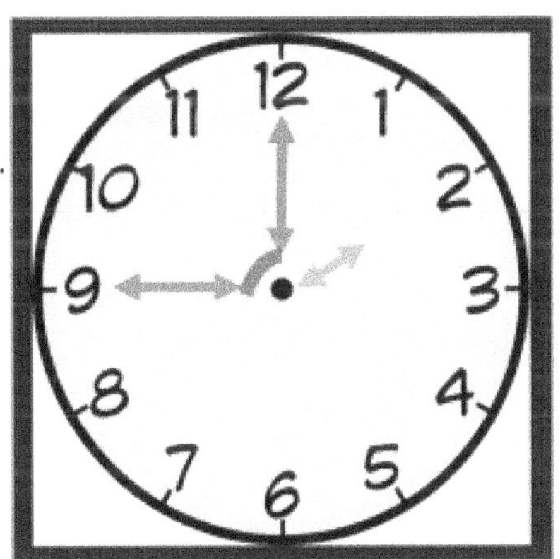

Hints and Tips

Leader and Follower face each other unless the Leader uses the framework to point the Follower in a different direction during the turn part of a move (eg blue arrow in diagram above).

A *Hockey Stick* is like an *Alemana* (underarm turn), but goes anti-clockwise instead of clockwise. The Leader raises his/her left hand (holding Follower's right), above the Leader's right shoulder (equi-distant between Leader and Follower).

The framework is open hold, Leader's left-hand grips Follower's right hand.

Move at right angles.

Travelling in a straight line means the Leader can lead better, and Follower make

Jive Basic Steps

Basic Step (Chasse and Rock Step)
Change of Place
Hand Behind the Back
Windmill

Jive Basic Steps

Foot work for all basic moves: Side to Side > Side to Side > Step back from partner > Rock forwards towards partner.

Suggested routine:

- *Basic Step.*
- *Change of Place.*
- *Hand Behind the Back.*
- *Windmill.*

Basic Step (Chasse and Rock Step)

The shape this move makes is like an 'L' lying on its side.

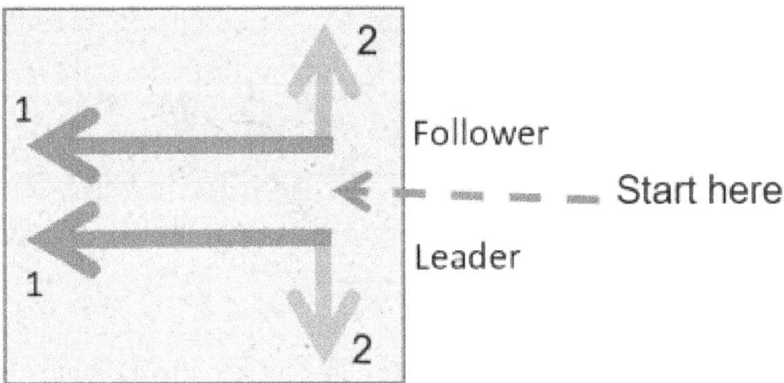

Leader: ((1) Stepping left along red arrow) side > Close > Side > (Stepping right along red arrow) side > Close > Side > ((2) Grey arrow) rock back > Step forward.

Follower: ((1) Stepping right along red arrow) side > Close > Side > (Stepping left along red arrow) side > Close > Side > ((2) Grey arrow) rock back > Step forward.

Change of Place

The shape this move makes is like a book being opened and closed.

Leader: (1) Side > Close > Side ((2) lift left arm to allow Follower to pass underneath, push Follower through with right hand) > Side > Close > Side > (3) Back > Replace > Side > Close > Side ((4) lift left arm to allow Follower to pass underneath, re-join in teapot framework) > (5) Side > Close > Side > (6) Back > Replace.

Follower: (1) Side > Close > Side ((2) 180 degree clockwise turn under Leader's raised arm to face partner again) > Side > Close > Side > (3) Back > Replace > Side > Close > Side ((4) 180 degree anti-clockwise turn under Leader's raised arm to face partner again) > (5) Side > Close > Side > (6) Back > Replace.

Hand Behind the Back

The shape this move makes is like a chair seat.

This is performed from a one-handed grip (Leader's left and Follower's right) instead of the usual teapot framework.

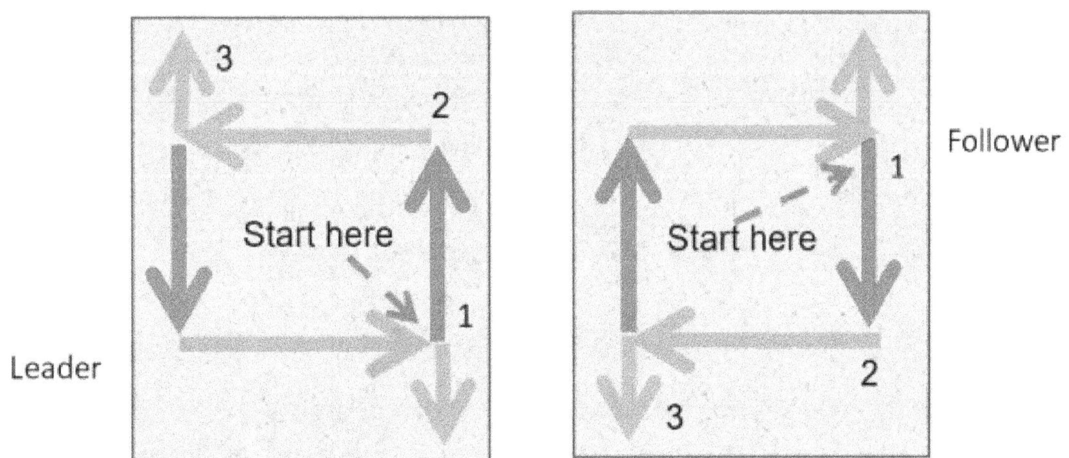

Leader and Follower: (1) Forward > Close > Forward > (Turn 90 degrees and pass hand around body then behind back) (2) Side > Close > Side > (3) Back > Replace > Repeat to return to starting position.

Windmill

The shape this move makes is like a squashed 'T'.

   This is performed from a two-handed grip instead of the usual teapot framework.

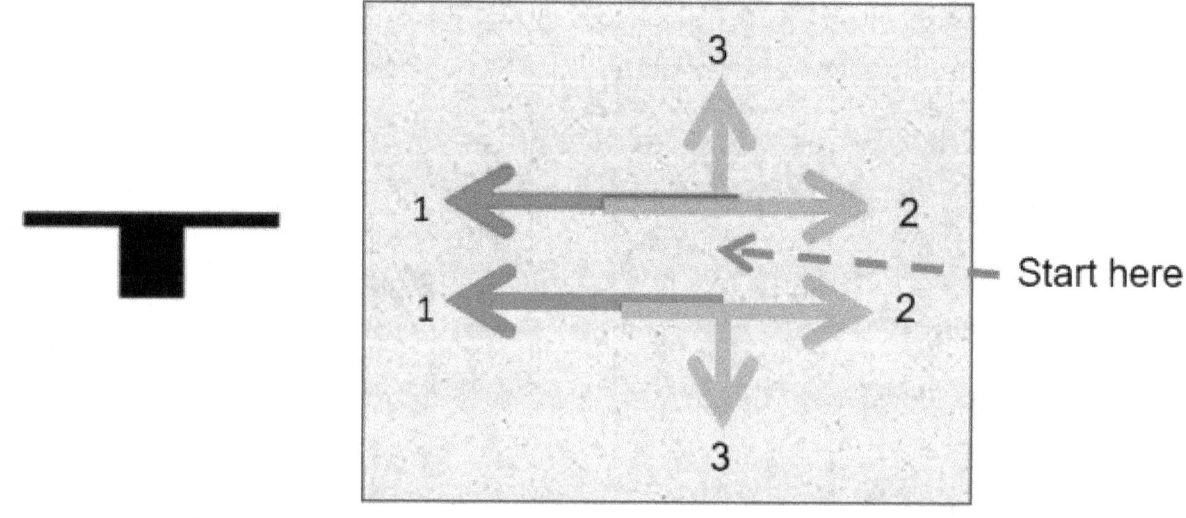

Leader and Follower: (1) Side > Close > Side > (2) Side > Close > Side > (3) Back > Replace.

How to Dance the Paso Doble

How to Dance the Paso Doble

Key principles:

- Walk in time to the music.
- Follow the line of dance ie go roughly corner to corner along a wall.
- Everything is done to a count of 8 beats. Start a new move when you get back to '1'.
- Suggested routine (below) follows the shape of a box. Use the 90 or 180 degree turns to either add a bit of style (to your travel around the room) or turn when you get to a corner.
- Dance as though you are a matador (Leader) flourishing a cape (Follower).

Steps for Leader and Follower	Timing (beats)
Step on spot	1 - 8
Side (to travel - Leader's right foot and Follower's left)	9
Close (Leader's left foot and Follower's right)	10
Side (to travel)	11
Close	12
Side (to travel)	13
Drag rear foot to closed position	14 - 16
Turn 180 degrees whilst stepping on spot	17 - 24
Stamp foot (Leader's right and Follower's left)	25
Walk forward (starting with Leader's left foot and Follower's right)	26 - 28
Leader walks backward whilst Follower walks forward	29 - 30
Side (to travel)	31
Close	32
Turn 90 degrees whilst stepping on spot > Start again	33 – 40

Rumba Basic Steps

Key Principles

Basic Step – Advanced Version

Rumba Basic Steps

Key principles for dancing the Rumba:

1) The steps are:

- Step.
- Rock.
- Slide (step and drag other foot to half closed position).

2) The basic steps rhythm is always 2, 3, 4, hold (don't move on beat 1). This can vary in more advanced moves.

Basic Step – Leader Steps Forward and Follower Backward

Follower Steps				P a u s e
Timing	2	3	4	1
Steps	Step	Rock weight onto opposite leg	Slide leg that has no weight on it	
Leader Steps				P a u s e

Basic Step – Leader Steps Backward and Follower Forward

Follower Steps				Pause
Timing	2	3	4	1
Steps	Step	Rock weight onto opposite leg	Slide leg that has no weight on it	Pause
Leader Steps				

The Rumba and Cha Cha Cha are essentially the same dance. See the Cha Cha Cha section for further details on how to do these moves.

Suggested routine:

- *Basic Step*.
- *New York*.
- *Basic Step*.
- *Hand to Hand*.
- *Alemana* (underarm turn).

You don't have to follow the moves in the order above, you can fit them together in different combinations.

Basic Step – Advanced Version

To get a more sensual movement in your dance (remember: Rumba is the dance of love), the timing can be changed to 2-and-3-and-4-and-1. This applies to both Leaders and Followers. Your Rumba will now be slightly faster and have more hip movement to make it look more like Salsa in style.

The Leader will look strong and proud. The Follower will look desirable and will spend the dance teasing (ie playing hard to get) the Leader who will be trying to win over the Follower.

Samba Basic Steps

Samba Basic Steps

Key principles for dancing the Samba:

1) Find your inner bounce.

2) The foundation steps are:

- Step (travelling).
- Bounce (on spot).
- Bounce (on spot).

3) The foundation rhythm is: Slow > Quick > Quick. Like a heartbeat: Dum, dum-dum.

To get yourself up and dancing the Samba just use: Step > Side > Close.

- The step is a small jump as though you are stepping over a 30cm hole in the ground.
- The Side > Close is on the spot where you land from the step.
- Rhythm: 1-a-2, 2-a-2.

Direction	Leader Steps	Follower Steps
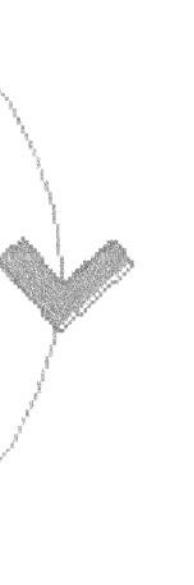	Forward and back in a straight line.	Forward and back in a straight line.

Round and round in anti-clockwise circle.

Straight forward, then turn roughly 45 degrees when going backwards. | Straight backwards, then turn roughly 45 degrees when going forward.

Side to side (known as a *Whisk*):

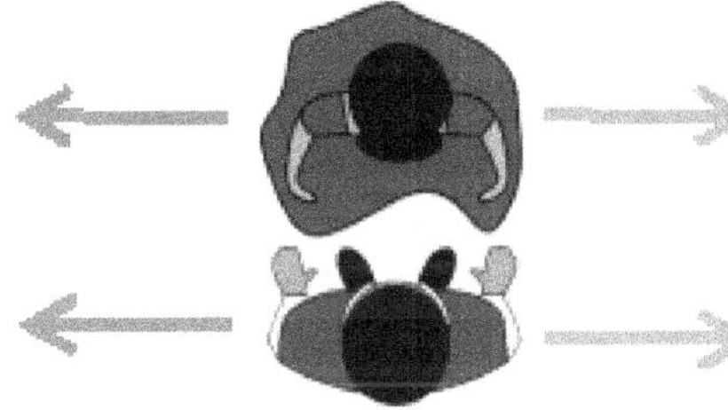

Sideways (left) > Step right foot behind left > Rock forward onto left foot > Sidestep right > Step left foot behind right > Rock forward onto right foot.

Sideways (right) > Step left foot behind right > Rock forward onto right foot > Sidestep left > Step right foot behind left > Rock forward onto left foot.

More advanced steps (eg *Samba Walk*) will require different footwork to the foundation steps

Thank you for reading the Goddard Method
of Latin Dancing.

This is an abridged version of the information in my book
(Goddard Method
of Ballroom and Latin Dancing) released for lockdown and as we
come out of it.

Available to buy* in hard copy or electronic format on Amazon
and Amazon Kindle.

*This publication is free through Kindle Unlimited.

Listed below is what you will find in the full book.

Chapter 1 Sharing my Dance Experiences and Introducing the Goddard Method of Ballroom and Latin Dancing

Chapter 2 Before You Start Dancing

Chapter 3 What is Dancing?

- How to Dance:
    - First Principles
    - Second Principles
- Direction of Travel
- Dance Framework

Chapter 4 Basic Ballroom Steps

- Waltz
- Viennese Waltz
- Quickstep
- Slow and Social Foxtrot
- Tango Basic

Chapter 5 Basic Latin Steps

- Cha Cha Cha
    - Basic Steps
    - Fan and Hockey Stick

- Jive
- Paso Doble
- Rumba
- Samba

Chapter 6 More Advanced Ballroom Steps

- Leading and Following
- Dance Positions
- Ballroom and Latin Dances – The Key Steps

- Double Reverse Spin – Waltz
- How to Dance Natural Pivots

Chapter 7 Technical Information

- The Benefits of Finding Someone With a Complementary Learning Style
- Sequence Versus Leading and Following
- Progressing From Beginner to Expert Dancer

Acknowledgements

Eve Moesiss

Thank you for your patience and attention to detail when illustrating the figures in this book.

About the Author

James Goddard

James has been dancing Ballroom and Latin for many years.

He also has experience of Salsa, Argentine Tango and Ceroc (Modern Jive).

James has an extensive interest in martial arts, which he has been practising for a number of years. He has experience of six martial arts spread over nine styles.

James noticed there were patterns and crossovers in principles of movement in martial arts. This is what inspired him to write his '*Goddard Method*' series of books.

If you liked this book, please look out for the *Goddard Method of Ballroom and Latin Dancing –* which has even more detail about how to dance. Also the *Goddard Method of Judo.* This will explain how to do judo in a similar style to the way James approached Latin in this book.

You can find out details about, and specials offers for, James' books on https://jamesgoddarddancing.wordpress.com

Did you love *Ellie's Magical Cat*? Then you should read *Judo: Throwing, Grappling and Striking* by James Goddard!

Judo is more than just throwing and grappling.

- It is helpful for a healthy mind and body.

- In an emergency it can be a useful aid for self-defence.

You can gain self-confidence and transferable skills for other disciplines such as ball games and dancing (sometimes known as fundamental movement skills).

This book is for beginners and experienced judo practitioners [judokas]. It can be referred to time and time again

Inside you will find:

- Easy to follow illustrations.

- Guidance on technique:

* Strikes and blocks.

* Throws.

* Kata.

* Holding techniques.

* Limb locking techniques.

* Strangles/chokes.

- Technical information on how to improve your judo as you gain experience helping you to feel and look great.

- Clear, helpful directions breaking details down into core techniques and variations.

My book aims to be the key that unlocks your understanding and potential so you can get the most out of lessons, books and YouTube presentations etc.

Other books concentrate on the technical side of judo, whereas my book emphasises the pattern/spirit in easy-to-remember key points, including a variety of applications.

Suitable as reference material for adaptive judo.

Most of this book is suitable for children and adults. Techniques are from the adult judo syllabus. Chapter 6 locking and strangling techniques are not shown in class to children under 12.

Read more at https://jamesgoddarddancing.wordpress.com/.

Also by James Goddard

Goddard Method
Goddard Method of Judo: Throwing, Grappling and Striking
Judo: Throwing, Grappling and Striking

Standalone
Partner Dancing: Ballroom and Latin
Ellie's Magical Cat

Watch for more at https://jamesgoddarddancing.wordpress.com/.

www.ingramcontent.com/pod-product-compliance
Lightning Source LLC
Chambersburg PA
CBHW060205120726
48004CB00007B/1698